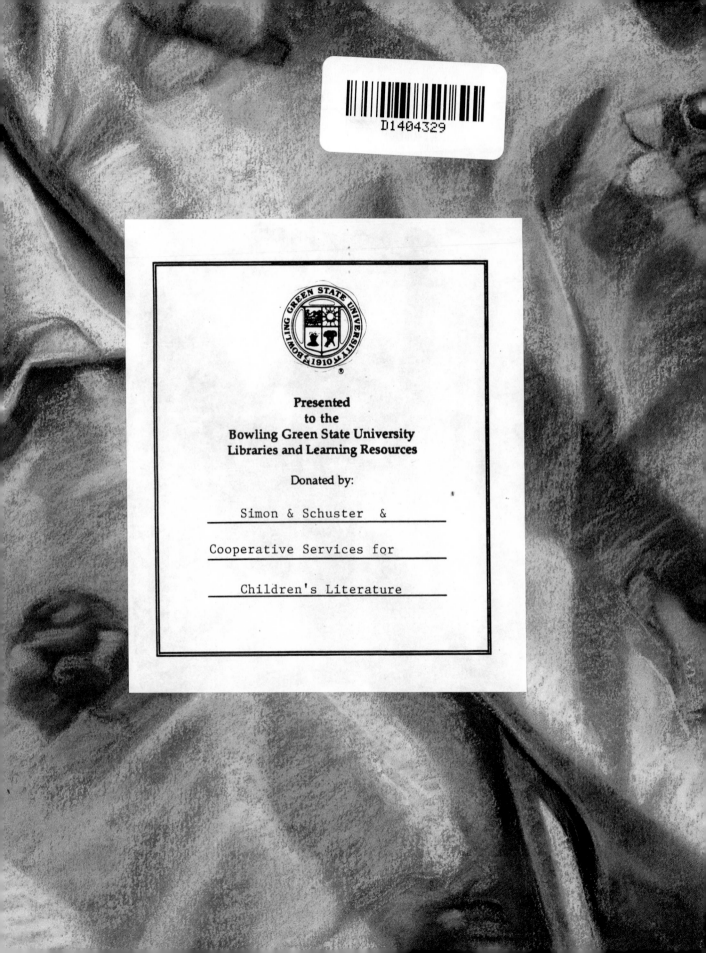

The Girl Who
Listened to Sinks

SIMON & SCHUSTER
BOOKS FOR YOUNG READERS

Published by Simon & Schuster

New York
London
Toronto
Sydney
Tokyo
Singapore

The Girl

Who Listened to Sinks

by JUSTINE RENDAL ▴ illustrated by REBECCA LEER

Once there was a little girl who could hear things talk. She listened to chairs and garbage pails, to carpets and bureaus. Pencils had interesting conversations among themselves but rarely talked to outsiders. Curtains often spoke in verse, hats were usually silly but charming, and necklaces were snobs.

Perhaps it was just as well that the girl could hear the conversations, for otherwise she might have been lonely. Her father had left and her mother was often rushed and impatient. The two of them lived in a dark apartment in a poor part of a rough city, where few people took the time to speak to children. The little girl went to a school with some mean kids who called her "Skinny Legs," and her mother had an awful job in an office with a boss who yelled.

They were only really happy for two weeks each summer, when they rented a tiny cottage by the shore. They took walks on the beach and made sand castles. On fine days they picnicked outside, and on rainy days she and her mother cuddled up on the porch and read stories to each other. The little girl listened to the conversation of the shells, as well as the sounds of the sea.

"Mother, can't we live by the sea always?" asked the little girl. "I wish we could live by the sea."

"I'm afraid not, and wishing doesn't make it so." Her mother sighed. "What would we live on? Do be practical. You are growing too old for dreaming."

The little girl tried not to be such a dreamer, but she still listened to the things that talked.

At night she brushed her hair a hundred strokes. "I am so tired!" complained the brush.

The little girl's arm was tired, too, but her mother was too tired to brush her daughter's hair. "Oh, I know it would be different if we lived by the sea," the girl told herself.

She lay down in her little white bed. "Good night," she whispered to the pillow.

"Good night," the pillow whispered back. "Sweet dreams."

Each night the girl dreamed of the sea. All night long the surf would sing joyfully and the foam would whisper secrets in her ear.

But in the mornings it was the dark little apartment again, and rush, rush, rush.

First it was time to make the bed.

"Ouch!" cried the sheet as the little girl pulled it taut.

"Sorry," she apologized, and slowed down.

"Who are you talking to?" asked her mother, but she didn't wait for an answer. "Hurry up, now."

The girl washed at the old, cracked sink in the bathroom. The sink was always glad to see her, but the cast-iron tub, the queen of the bathroom, was always very cold. The girl dressed herself beside the sink and even tried to do her own hair. It was difficult to make a good ponytail without help, and her ribbon got knotted in the elastic.

"Mother, would you tie my bow?" asked the little girl.

"I don't have time!" snapped her mother. "Now hurry up or you'll make me late for work. Oh, I hate my job. It is boring, boring, boring. But I can't afford to lose it."

They went out together into the rush-hour crowd.

On the bus, as the girl put her money in the fare box, she heard it complain to the coins. "Stop rushing, always rushing. One at a time, please. A little decorum, if you don't mind."

"Mother, what is decorum?" asked the little girl.

"It's manners," said her mother. "Where do you get these strange words from?" By then it was time to push through the crowd and get off the bus.

Each morning the little girl awakened from her dreams of the sea and went into the bathroom to wash and brush her teeth at the old, cracked sink.

"Oh, boy! Here she comes," cried the toothbrush. "Time to get scrubbing!"

"Good morning," said the little girl politely as she picked it up.

"Oh, that tickles!" giggled the toothpaste tube as the little girl gently squeezed it.

Only the mirror wasn't cheerful. "Boring, boring, boring," it complained. "Always the same people to reflect. Will things never change?"

The little girl made some faces at it, hoping that would make the mirror happy.

The tub criticized everything and had convinced the sink it was ugly. "If only I wasn't," said the sink, sighing.

"Oh, you're not so bad," said the mat, which, unlike most rugs, wasn't full of resentment.

"That is one mat's opinion," said the bathtub, sniffing. She was very proud of her own looks, especially her legs and her feet, which were shaped like lion's claws. "Some are stuck with skinny legs. Not everyone can have legs like mine."

"Yes, it's my legs," agreed the poor sink. "They *are* horrid."

"Well, perhaps a skirt would help," suggested the bathtub. "It would cover up some of your figure problems."

"A skirt!" exclaimed the sink. "Of course! I'm sure I'd feel lovely in a skirt!"

"A skirt wouldn't hurt," rhymed the curtain.

"Oh, how I wish I had a skirt," said the sink, sighing.

"If wishes were horses, beggars would ride," said the bathtub nastily. "Wishing doesn't make it so."

"What's taking you so long in the bathroom?" cried the girl's mother from the hall. "We'll be late."

"I was listening to the sink," answered the little girl.

"Well, stop it right now!" her mother said. "We have to go. And stop all this nonsense about things talking. You are far too old for such silliness."

But all that day in school the little girl could not stop thinking about the poor sink. Her teacher yelled at her for daydreaming.

"I shall just have to get the sink a skirt," decided the little girl at last. "That will fix things."

The next day she took all of her savings (which was not very much) and went to a fancy dress shop. "I want a skirt," she told the saleslady.

"I'm afraid we don't have skirts in *your* size," said the lady, who didn't look afraid at all. "And besides, *our* skirts are very expensive."

"It's not for me. It's for a friend. And I only need half a skirt because she always leans against the wall."

The saleslady made an angry face. "I have no time for games, little girl. Out of the shop with you!"

"Well, it can't be hard to make a skirt," thought the little girl, who had sewn clothes for her dolls. She went to a store full of beautiful fabrics.

"How much for that pink material with flowers?" asked the girl.

"How much do you need?" asked the shopkeeper.

"Well, it's for a forty-five-inch-around skirt."

"You will need three yards. And perhaps you need some elastic for the waist and some lace for trim."

The girl agreed that she would, and had just enough money left over to buy a pink satin sash, as well. "I think it will suit the sink," she thought.

The next day the girl carefully cut the fabric. Then she pinned it. She was alone at home after school, but she didn't feel lonely because the pins kept chattering like a crowd of girls at a dance: "What is she making?" "I think it's for a party." "Maybe a ball!" "Oh, I hope she forgets to take me out of the skirt and I get to go!"

The girl pushed the needle in and out, in and out. "My job is so dull. Boring, boring, boring," said the needle.

The girl felt sorry for it. Sewing the skirt took days and days, but she kept at it each afternoon when she was home alone. By Saturday it was done.

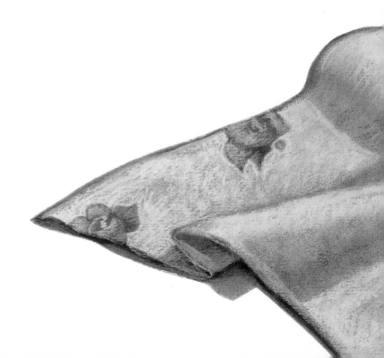

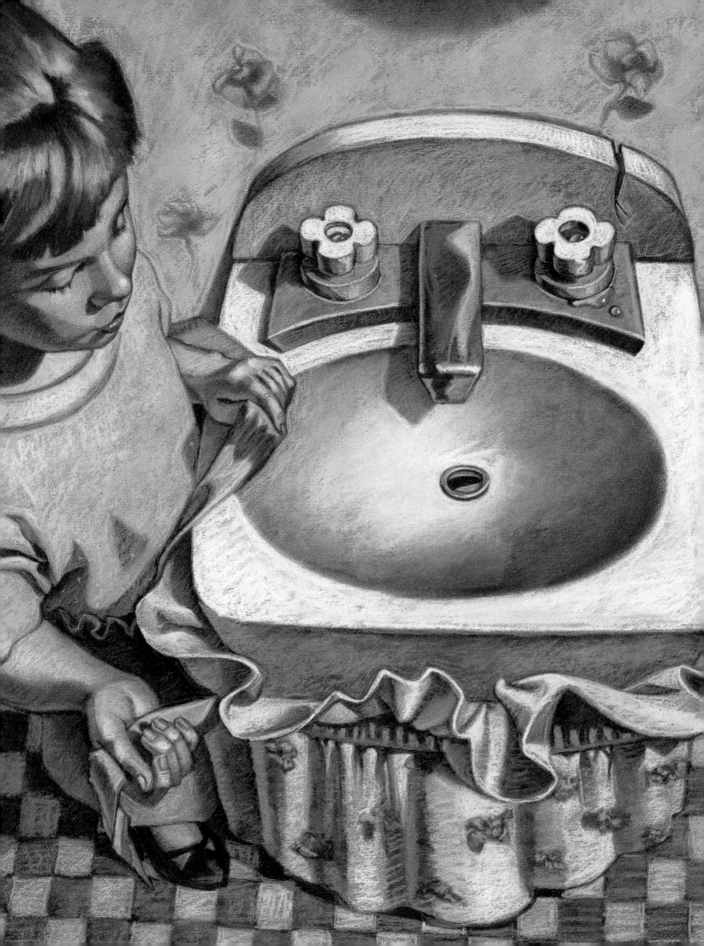

The little girl took the skirt into the bathroom and spread it around the sink.

"Oh, my. Oh, my. I think I may cry!" cried the sink. "Isn't it beautiful! How do I look?" she asked.

"You look lovely," said the mat.

"Really?" asked the sink shyly.

"Indeed," said the mirror. "Look here."

"Not bad," admitted the bathtub.

"So that is what you have been so busy doing," said the girl's mother. She looked the skirt over carefully. "Very nice," she said.

"My, what a good idea that sink skirt is!" said a neighbor who visited. "Could you make one for me, dear? I would be happy to pay you for it."

"Certainly," said the girl, and she made one in blue with polka dots.

The two skirts became the talk of the building, then of the neighborhood. Dozens of people asked for them.

"Certainly," said the little girl, who liked to make both people and sinks happy.

Her mother began to help her sew. After a while they were so busy that her mother quit work and stayed home and made sink skirts. It was nice for the little girl to come home from school and find her mother there, happily sewing. Soon they hired a lady to help sew, and then another.

Sinks around the country rejoiced. Orders rolled in.

Wealthy people wanted silk skirts. Business people ordered tailored skirts. Athletes wanted sporty models; models wanted slinky ones. There was a Scarlet O'Hara style for southern sinks, a Betsy Ross for patriotic sinks. There was even a hula skirt (which for a short time became the craze in Newton, Massachusetts).

But most little girls wanted pink ones with ruffles.

"Business is booming, but I am not sure we can keep up with all these orders," said the girl's mother one evening, as they sat amid the taffeta scraps and dotted swiss snippets.

"Shall we hire more help?" asked the girl.

"We don't have enough room here as it is!" replied her mother.

"Well, perhaps we shall have to move," said the girl. She smiled at her mother. "Would you like to brush my hair?" she asked.

"Certainly," said her mother.

The business kept growing.

"I'll scream if one more person steps on me!" growled the carpet.

"Oh, keep it to yourself!" hissed the radiator.

"Look at all that has changed!" said the sink, smiling.

"Now I'm busy all day," chuckled the mirror. "And such interesting faces to reflect."

"Well, she'll get too big and then she'll leave us. She'll pack up, move on, and forget her old friends. See if she doesn't," said the bathtub.

"Oh, no!" cried the sink. "She wouldn't leave *me* now."

"Yes, she'll move on, and when she does, she'll probably take your skirt, too," said the bathtub spitefully.

That night, instead of the song of the sea, the little girl heard the sink weeping.

People heard about the little girl and her success. A newspaper sent someone to interview her and take her picture after school.

"How did you ever think of sink skirts?" asked the reporter.

"I didn't really. The bathtub did, and then the sink wanted one because it had skinny legs. I just listened to the sink," said the little girl.

"Have you always wanted to be rich?" asked the reporter.

"I didn't do it for the money. I did it for the sink," explained the girl. "Still, I enjoy the money just the same."

The next day newspaper headlines read THE GIRL WHO LISTENS TO SINKS GETS RICH. Most people thought the little girl was just being modest. Her mother, however, was not so sure.

Things had certainly changed. The teachers at school were very polite to the little girl, and the other students stopped teasing her and wanted to be friends.

"I didn't really think your legs were skinny," said one of the mean girls. "Want to come to my house after school?" she asked.

"Mother, do we have a lot of money now? Are we really rich?" asked the little girl when she got home that afternoon.

"Well, I have not had time to count it, but I think we may be. What shall we do with all the money?"

"Shall we buy a house by the sea?" asked the little girl. "We could have a workroom for our sewing, and I could go to a nice new school; and we could have picnics and walk on the beach together."

"What a good idea!" said her mother.

"And we'll take the sink with us."

"Another good idea!"

"But we'll leave the bathtub behind."

So they found a perfect house with both a sun porch and a shade porch, a big room for sewing, and two bedrooms. The little girl's bedroom had a round window that looked out over the sea. Both the girl and her mother were very happy.

"I am sorry I told you not to listen to sinks," said the little girl's mother, who was really not a mean person but who had only been frightened and nervous and tired and rushed. "Now we are both happy because you *did* listen."

"When we get to our new home, shall we take a walk on the beach?" asked the little girl, who was already listening to the song of the sea.

To Paul, in the bathtub —JR

To my mother and sister,
with special thanks to Lacey and Lisa —RL

SIMON & SCHUSTER BOOKS FOR YOUNG READERS
Simon & Schuster Building, Rockefeller Center
1230 Avenue of the Americas, New York, New York 10020
Text copyright © 1993 by Justine Rendal. Illustrations copyright © 1993 by Rebecca Leer.
All rights reserved including the right of reproduction in whole or in part in any form.
SIMON & SCHUSTER BOOKS FOR YOUNG READERS is a trademark of Simon & Schuster.

Designed by David Neuhaus.
The text of this book is set in Stempel Garamond.
The illustrations were done in pastels.
Manufactured in the United States of America   10 9 8 7 6 5 4 3 2 1

Library of Congress Cataloging-in-Publication Data
Rendal, Justine.
   The girl who listened to sinks / by Justine Rendal: illustrated
by Rebecca Leer.   Summary: A young girl's ability to talk to inanimate objects leads
to a better life for her and her mother, who both want to live by
the sea.   [1. Mothers and daughters—Fiction.]   I. Leer, Rebecca. ill.
II. Title.   PZ7.R2847Gi 1993 [E]—dc20 91-42900 CIP
ISBN 0-671-77745-9

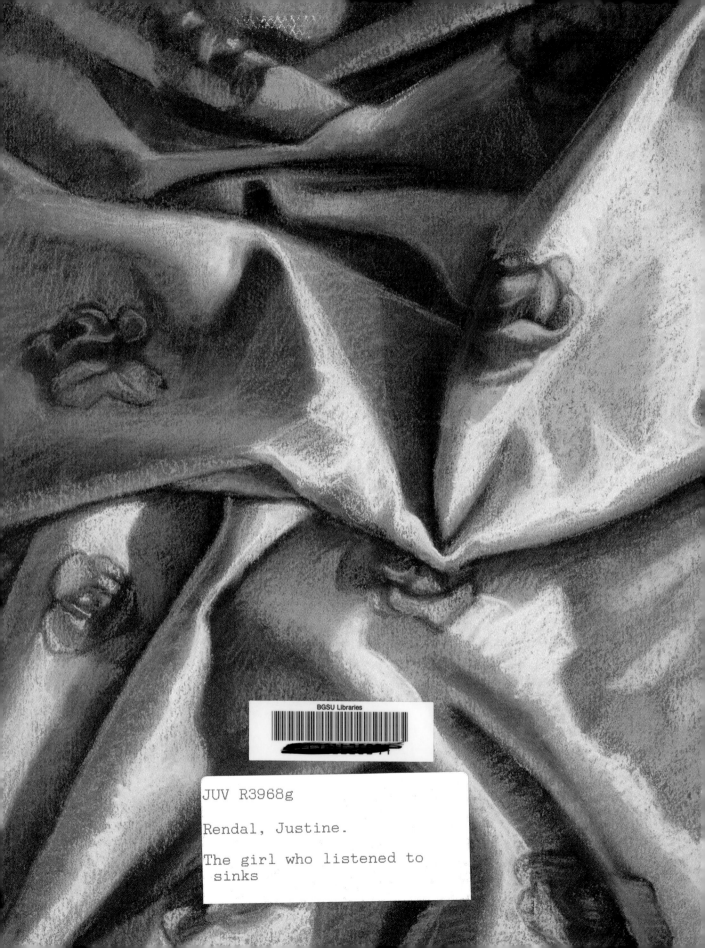